Hello, World, You're Mine?

Hello, World, You're Mine?

by Winifred Rouse Simpson
Illustrated by Michael Hackett

Publishing House
St. Louis

Copyright © 1987 Concordia Publishing House
3558 S. Jefferson Avenue, St. Louis, MO 63118-3968
Manufactured in the United States of America

Library of Congress Cataloging in Publication Data
Simpson, Winifred Rouse, 1937–
        Hello, world, you're mine?

        (The Christian reader)
        Summary: A homecoming queen struggles with pride and its effects on her faith and personal relationships after suffering an accident.
        [1. Christian life—Fiction] I. Title.   II. Series.
PZ7.S609He   1987   [Fic]   86-31734
ISBN 0-570-03643-7 (pbk.)

---

1 2 3 4 5 6 7 8 9 10   IB   96 95 94 93 92 91 90 89 88 87

To Holly Danielle

Dearest Holly,

I wrote this story for you. This is why I must thank you for your loving patterns which helped so much in the telling of this story. One day I hope you'll understand what I am trying to say, and know that above all else I shall always be

Your affectionate (Fairy) Godmother,
Auntie Win

Contents

*Pride goes before destruction,
a haughty spirit before a fall.
Proverbs 16:18*

1
The
Homecoming
Queen

Fall, my favorite season, would be extra special this year. The late November afternoon was warm and golden, trees were a riot of color, and the last minutes of class were dragging.

When the bell announced Thanksgiving break on Wednesday, Hill View Junior Academy went wild! Everyone was shoving and shouting to friends down the crowded corridor, anxious to be free. Kelliann Lang's giggle always came first.

Then I saw the bright flash of her copper hair. Kelliann was one of the beautiful people . . . a bit loud, but still, I thought, *beautiful*.

Stepping into the crowd, I stretched my stride to match hers as she grinned down at me, saying, "Let's go, little Homecoming Queen!"—and my heart raced at the thought.

Homecoming queen was something I really wanted. Kids even smiled at me in the hall, but I wouldn't find out if I'd won the vote until Friday evening. The school newspaper staff would count the ballots, and the winner would be honored at the football game on Saturday. But lots of other pretty girls were in the contest—including Kelliann—and I wondered . . .

"Do I really have a chance?"

"Hollis Manning!" Kelliann uses my full name when she's making a point. "As head cheerleader, you've got it made for . . . UH!" she grunted as someone bumped us hard from behind.

My books slapped the floor, papers slithered under trampling feet, and I groaned when I saw my term paper scattering.

Sally Whittle smirked as she dashed past.

"Better watch it, Holly," she taunted. "All brains, no grace!"

Kelliann's green eyes narrowed. "Wacko jerk!" she yelled so as to be heard above the slamming of metal locker doors.

My cheeks were burning. I knew Sally was mad because I got an A on the math quiz. It wasn't the first time my grades had caused me trouble, but the hurt got deeper each time.

Wendell Bressler handed me two smudged sheets. "Sorry," he mumbled. "They've been stepped on, Holly."

Before I could answer, Hank Masterson shoved Wendell aside, shouting, "Move it, lame-brain! I've got football practice." Hank grinned at me and lowered his voice. "As the team captain, I take the queen to the Christmas Sno-Ball party, Holly."

Hank's our star quarterback, so I should've been pleased. Only Wendell was struggling to keep his glasses from falling off, Kelliann was yelling at me to hurry, and all at once a salty taste filled my mouth and I felt the tears wanting to come. Normally, I don't cry, but lately the least little thing turns me on like a faucet. *Please, God,* I prayed, *don't let me cry. Not now!* Thanking Wendell, I hurried to catch Kelliann before the heavy door swung closed.

She tugged on one ear, saying, "All the better to hear you with, my dear!" making fun of Wendell as I joined her.

"At least *he* helped me," I snapped.

"So? What's the matter with you, kid?" She raised one eyebrow at me. "Wendell's a nothing—yes?"

I thought, *No, this time I don't agree with you.* But I didn't say it out loud. Going along with Kelliann gave me a feeling of belonging. The nickname 'kid' meant she liked me. But I'd felt so weird lately, I wasn't so sure about things anymore.

"Give!" she said, nudging my arm as we walked toward home. "What's up anyway?"

"Sally won't vote for me, and . . . "

"Forget her," she cut in. "With teeth like that Sally'll never be queen of anything." Kelliann's red waves shimmered as she tossed her head and raised her chin defiantly.

We stopped under the big maple tree in my front yard. The leaves had already turned. I looked up into a mass of gold while she rambled on about queens, cheerleaders, and being popular. Kelliann was talking about having my picture in the paper when I decided to change the subject. "I read about a tree like this once," I said. "It's my raintree. If you stand under a golden tree and make a wish, it's gotta come true. If you had a wish, what would you want, Kelliann?"

"Mmm. Almond fudge is my favorite ice cream."

Kelliann's eyes flashed like emeralds. "Get serious," I said, wondering what I'd look like with green eyes instead of dark brown. "For my wish, I'd like to know why Sally and Kim Peters always smirk at me."

Kelliann tucked her front teeth over her bottom lip and giggled. "And *they'd* wish for your wavy black hair and straight teeth. C'mon, kid. Cheer up. Let's hear your good luck saying for being the next homecoming queen."

"Hello, world, you're mine!" I said firmly, feeling a tingle of excitement shiver through me. I'd said that for luck when we'd started junior high. It had worked, too. But this was eighth grade, my last year, and things were getting too complicated.

"That's the spirit," she called, dancing away

down the sidewalk. "Let's go practice that pyramid again."

"Go ahead while I check in," I called, running for the porch. "Aunt Dede's here while my parental units are in the Bahamas for their anniversary." We both laughed at the name I'd given my parents, Kelliann's giggle echoing as the screen door banged behind me.

Aunt Dede's note was on the kitchen table. She was doing volunteer work at the hospital again. On the bottom of her note, I scribbled where I was going and then dashed outside for another look at my golden raintree.

Should I wish—pray—for homecoming queen? For as long as I could remember, people had been making a fuss over my looks. "Such a cute, tiny figure!" they'd say, or "What a lovely complexion." Why would God have made me so pretty if He didn't want me to use my terrific looks? It was fun being in the middle of things. If being queen meant being popular, then that was God's plan for me. After all, didn't Jesus say that He came so that we "may have life, and have it to the full"?

Kelliann's probably right, I thought as I ran

toward the school field. Sally and Kim are just jealous. All the way I kept repeating, "Hello, world, you're mine!"

When I got to the field the cheerleaders were standing around in little groups, whispering. "What's up?" I called.

Sally spun around, drawing back her lips in a horrid grin to show off a wad of silver braces stuck to her teeth. "Didn't you hear?" she asked snidely. In our small town, news usually spreads fast.

"Hear what?"

"The sirens for one thing," Kim Peters replied. She was tying a headband around her mousy, fly-away hair. "Corin Reinfeld burned down her garage. Now she can't be in the queen contest."

"Not that you'd care!" Sally added.

They put their heads together again, giggling.

Sneering at them over one shoulder, I turned away, swirling my pleated skirt high. Dad said I had cute legs, much nicer than Kim's at least. Her knees rubbed together, and she had fat ankles. If they had a problem, so what? I wasn't going to let them hurt me.

Thank You, Jesus, I prayed, *for making me*

prettier than Kim and Sally. With your help, Lord, I'll be homecoming queen even without their votes. Then they'll be sorry for being so nasty. And thank You, Jesus, for loving me so much.

Praying made me feel good. God was on my side. He'd given me great looks, and I'd trust Him to show me how to be a pretty Christian.

2
The
Accident

Kelliann was talking to Hank when I got to the bench. The minute she saw me, she squealed, "Can you believe it? That Corin's a real loser—for sure!"

"How'd it happen?" I asked.

Hank flashed one of his dimpled grins. "She was sneaking a smoke," he said. Then he jogged over to the supply shack to join the rest of the team, shaking his head and chuckling to himself.

I didn't see anything funny about smoking, and all at once I felt like crying again. What was the matter with me? Did it have anything to do with the way Sally and Kim were acting? I wasn't sure. Flopping on the bench beside Kelliann, I asked, "Do you ever feel—well—sort of lonely inside?"

She eyed me suspiciously, then burst into a fit of giggles. "Are you nuts? How can I possibly be lonely in a house with two older sisters and only one bathroom?"

That wasn't funny either, I thought. Why couldn't I ever talk to Kelliann? I wanted to share the way I felt. But how can you share something when you don't know what to share, and no one will truly listen? I was staring at puffy clouds sailing over the trees when Hank yelled. He and the guys were horsing around with some of the other sports equipment in the shack, and he wanted me to watch.

"Showoff," I muttered.

"Yeah, but cute," Kelliann said.

When Hank yelled again, I stood up and squinted. "What's he doing? He reminds me of one of those guys in the summer Olympics. Why is he all bent over like that?"

Kelliann giggled. But when she said, "He's

20

throwing the discus," her expression was one of pure worship.

There was a bright flash. Suddenly something hit me . . . a piece of steel? The discus? I sat down hard, dazed for a second. Then Hank was there. "Are you okay, Holly?"

" 'Course I am, I . . . " I shoved my hair back from my face. There was blood on my fingers. "Oh, I'm bleeding," I said. Stupidly obvious! It was embarrassing to have them gawking at me.

Things began blurring; kids came running; there was a lot of shoving; and the ambulance came swishing onto the field.

"This is silly," I said. "I'm not hurt"—and all the time blood kept oozing down my cheek. A man from the rescue squad kept pushing my hand out of the way and pressing gauze against my face.

"Where are we going?" I asked as they put me on a stretcher.

Someone shouted, "Lie down!"

I was vaguely aware of the dreadful ride—I was glad to be lying down, after all—and the glare of hospital lights, and Dr. Costabile, and Aunt Dede with a worried expression, and the choking smell of antiseptic, and the sting of orange foam, and the stitches going in—far too many of them, I thought—and Dr. Costabile driving me home and speaking softly when he gave me a shot so I would sleep, which I did even before Aunt Dede turned out the lights.

3
The Scar

When I woke up, bright sunshine was making golden puddles on my quilt. Still dazed, I thought about school, forgetting it was Thanksgiving Day. When I tried to get up, a dozen aches stabbed me from every direction. My head felt like it was about to roll onto the floor any minute. Very slowly, I made it to the bathroom and the mirrored wall above the sink.

I nearly keeled over on the spot. Both eyes were swollen almost shut. There was a large purplish bump on my forehead, and the whole side of my face was bandaged like the mummy's revenge.

"AUNT DEDE!" I shrieked at the top of my lungs.

She must've been waiting in the hall, 'cause I never knew she could move that fast. "It's okay, honey," she said, too cheerfully. "You're very lucky. That was quite a blow you took, but nothing is broken. Dr. Costabile said you'll be just fine."

Right then I knew things were *not* fine. Grown-ups have a way of saying things to make you feel good, while inside you know the real truth. "What about the queen contest?" I mumbled from inside gauze and tape.

"There'll be other contests," she said, tucking me back in bed. "Right now you need to rest. Are you hungry?"

Terrific! My world had just collapsed, and Aunt Dede wanted to feed my stomach. She returned from the kitchen with a tall glass of eggnog—I couldn't chew, but I could swallow—and a tiny vase of roses from Hank's family. Queens get roses, but I'd never be a queen now.

"What's under this?" I asked, pointing to the wad on my face. I could vaguely remember a lot of stitches going in.

"Dr. Costabile was very careful, Holly. I'm sure there won't be much of a scar."

SCAR! Would you listen to that? How can anyone live with half her face missing? *Why, God? I prayed. How could You let this happen to me? You're supposed to be on my side!*

I spent Thanksgiving weekend in my room staring at striped wallpaper covered with pink roses. I began to hate roses. And I sure didn't have anything to be thankful for, either. Someone from school called to tell Aunt Dede that I'd won the vote for queen, but I couldn't even go to the game! Kelliann was runner-up and took my place, but something knotted in my stomach. Somehow I felt betrayed. Hank called, but I wouldn't talk to him.

On Wednesday Aunt Dede drove me to Dr. Costabile to have the stitches taken out. I couldn't go back to school until he'd examined my face. "Hank is very sorry," Aunt Dede said, gripping the steering wheel firmly. "I wish you'd talk to him. He said his father's insurance will take care of everything."

"Isn't that nice?" I said, trying to sound offhand.

"Won't you let him apologize? You've been friends for a long time, and it *was* an accident."

"Accident! That total jerk! How can he apologize for battering my face?"

Aunt Dede's mouth puckered, but she didn't say anything. We drove the rest of the way in silence. That suited me just fine. I certainly didn't want to talk about that stupid show-off. For a football hero, Hank was sure a zero to me. If he hadn't tried throwing that discus—which he had no business doing—I would've been homecoming queen. Not Kelliann. I hated him. In fact, I never wanted to see Hank again for as long as I lived.

Dr. Costabile was gentle, but his tugging on the stitches made my cheek burn. "It's coming along nicely, Hollis," he said, bragging about his handiwork. "Now we'll leave the dressing off. It will heal better that way. Unless there are complications, you'll be able to go back to school on Monday."

Complications? My whole life was a mess. The scar was red and horrible. I wanted to crawl into a hole somewhere and hide. Mom and Dad were enjoying a sandy beach while I shriveled into an old hag, and they didn't care. Nobody cared!

When Kelliann came over that evening, I watched her face when she saw my cheek.

"It's positively gross," I said. "How can I go to the Christmas Sno-Ball party like this?"

It would've been nice if she had said it didn't look too bad. Instead, Kelliann put on her best polite expression and said, "Takes time, kid. Besides, the Sno-Ball dance is two weeks away. You'll be okay by then."

"No I won't! Don't you understand? I'm scarred for life. How can a scar-face go to a school dance? I'd be so embarrassed I'd just . . . just die!"

Kelliann lowered her eyes. "The eighth-grade dance is really special," she murmured softly. "I'll miss you."

"You're not going, are you?" My mouth felt dry and awful, like a whole troop of scouts had just tramped across my tongue. I was so sure she wouldn't go without me, but she just shrugged.

"It's my first dance, kid. I didn't think you'd mind."

But I did mind! We did all our "firsts" together. I didn't listen when she started telling me about her dress. How could she treat me like this? Kelliann was supposed to be my best friend. I was just staring at her when her words came through. " . . . so I'll stop over and bring your homework. Yes?"

"Wh-what?" She'd really confused my brain.

One of her tawny eyebrows went up—I couldn't do that—and she giggled. "Well, I didn't think you'd be going back to school right away. Do you mind if I volunteer to take your part in the Christmas pageant? I could learn the dance steps and . . . "

"No!" I yelled. "First, you take homecoming queen. Now you're going to the party without me— and you dance like a clod! And now you want my part in the pageant! Go away, you . . . you . . . I hate you. I don't want to see you. Ever again!"

Tears blinded me as I streaked toward my room. I could hear Aunt Dede talking quietly to Kelliann, then the front door close, but I kept on pounding my pillow. It was unfair. God had deserted me! He'd made me pretty, then He'd taken back His gift just when I needed it the most.

"Not-fair-not-fair-not-fair!"

Aunt Dede came in and sat on the edge of my bed. "Oh, Holly," she said softly. "It's not the end of the world, honey. The doctor said it would take time, but the scar will go away."

"Doctors just *say* that stuff," I sobbed. "No one will ever talk to me again. I'm ruined—forever!"

4
The Place to Hide

Monday morning I came to the kitchen in my bathrobe. Aunt Dede glanced at the clock as she took hot biscuits from the oven, and said, "It's late. Shouldn't you be dressed for school?"

"I'm not going," I announced firmly. "The kids will gawk."

"Oh, pish!" she said with a snort. "People have better things to do than stare at you, Hollis Manning."

I couldn't believe it! Where was the gentle Auntie who'd always cared so much about me? I was looking at her with my mouth open when she whipped away my plate of eggs.

"I'll keep this warm while you dress," she said. "I don't need you under my feet all day."

It hurt to discover that my little Auntie was made of iron with a dash of hot sauce for flavoring. She must not like me very much after all.

Before I left for school, she called me into the bathroom. "Let's brush your hair to one side like this," she said, sweeping a curl across my ugly cheek. "The windblown look is very chic these days."

Who was thinking about fashion? I was dreading the thought of facing everyone in school.

That week was awful. People didn't stare at me openly, but whenever I passed a group they'd get very quiet. News at Hill View spreads faster than measles. Sally came up to me in homeroom one morning—I was sitting in the back row—and asked if I'd help her with the decimals for the math posters. "Maybe now you aren't too stuck up to help," she added.

Stuck-up? Where'd she get that dumb idea? I

just turned my back on Sally and didn't answer. I might be ugly, I thought, but I still have feelings.

By the end of that week, frost had shriveled the golden leaves on my raintree. My spirits did a nosedive. "Hello, world," I whispered to myself, "you're sure not mine anymore." God hadn't wanted me to be pretty in the first place, and that made me feel empty inside. I guess I must have done something that Jesus didn't want to forgive after all.

When I got to my room, I found a strange book on my bed. I went to ask Aunt Dede about it. She looked up from a pile of Christmas cards she was addressing and peered at me over her glasses. "It looks like a journal to me," she said. "I bought it for you this afternoon."

"What for?" I wanted to know.

"As long as you're reveling in self-pity, I thought you'd like to take notes. It helps to write down your feelings. When things get back to normal you can read what you wrote and have a good laugh at yourself."

"There's nothing funny about being scarred for life!" I shouted. "Can't you understand that?"

"I understand you're being ridiculous, Hollis," she said in a severe tone. "There are many in this world who are in far worse condition than you."

It's a good thing I know when to keep my mouth shut. I was so mad at her right then I wanted to scream. Why should I care about other people? They weren't *me!*

Tuesday morning I went to see my advisor, Mr. Anders, about choosing my classes for the next semester. He's a cool guy; all the kids like him. He kept tugging on his neat little beard while we talked.

"Science is a good choice, Hollis," he said. "That will prepare you for biology in high school. What about your elective?"

I shrugged, and told him I hadn't thought about it. I'd already given up cheerleading.

"Have you thought about the school newsletter?"

I said, "No," because I'd always been too busy before the accident. I'd forgotten that Mr. Anders was the advisor for our paper, *The Hill View Review*.

"We meet in the art room," he continued.

"They're great kids, and we have a lot of fun. Why not stop by? We always need someone to run copies for us. The only time we can use the mimeograph is after school."

That's when my brain started working overtime. If I stayed after school on a project, Aunt Dede couldn't needle me. The copy machine was in the library, the one spot most of the kids I knew avoided like the plague. What a great way to hide my ugly face.

That afternoon Mr. Anders showed me around. He explained how to set the mimeograph, then told me about the files which he called a "morgue." "It was organized before school started," he said, frowning. "Could you straighten things out for me? Order out of chaos is the idea, Hollis."

Working in a morgue certainly fit my mood. I told him I'd try, then spent the rest of the day on the file folders. The library was deliciously quiet, too.

On Wednesday I found Aunt Dede waiting for me when I left the school. That was odd, since I usually walked home.

"What's wrong?" I asked, opening the car door.

"Get in," she said. "There's someone I want you to meet."

We drove in silence, then drove into the parking lot under the children's hospital. All sorts of questions tickled my mind, but I decided not to say anything. Aunt Dede was wearing one of her determined looks—which meant trouble. Taking the elevator to the sixth floor blue wing, she hauled me quickly into a dressing room and tied a volunteer's apron over my school clothes. I followed her down a shiny hallway that smelled of disinfectant and medication. There was something scary about the muffled sounds around me, I thought, and decided this was a sad place. When Aunt Dede stopped before the swinging doors at the end of the hall, I was suddenly afraid.

"His name is Michael," she whispered. "When he was nine, his house caught fire. His father died saving him. Michael is your age, but he has endured a lot of pain. He was a very beautiful child, Holly." The way she said it made my heart thump.

Then Aunt Dede took my hand and together we pushed through the doors into the solarium.

5
The Creature Behind the Painting

At first I thought the large room was empty. There was an easel near the wall of glass overlooking Hill View Memorial Park. Behind it something moved. When I saw the head poke around the edge of the canvas, my knees started shaking. For a minute I thought I was going to be sick. Aunt Dede marched me right up to this ugly thing and brightly said, "Hello, Michael. I brought Holly to see your painting."

His fat lips twisted into a sneering smile. Thick eyelids drooped, and the shiny bald head nodded. "It's almost finished," he rasped.

I looked away to the picture and was surprised. Brilliant yellow swirled across an azure sky. Bright red poppies dotted a grassy hill above a stretch of rocky beach. In one corner lay a sea shell, delicately painted in peach and coral. "It's . . . beautiful," I stammered.

"Do you really like it?" he croaked. "I love the beach. I like to swim, too. Do you swim, Holly?"

Swallowing hard, I nodded. But I didn't dare take my eyes off that painting. If I did, I'd have to look at him again. Groping for something to say, I asked, "Do you take art lessons—uh . . . ?" "My name is Michael," he said softly. "No, I don't take lessons. I just like painting. What do you like to do?"

It was hard to breathe. "I . . . I love writing stories." It surprised me that I'd admitted my secret love for writing to a stranger. I kept staring at the poppies in his painting until, I thought, it looked like they were moving with a gentle sea breeze.

"I'll bet you're good," he whispered, touching my hand.

Tears burned in my eyes. I wanted to run, to hide, to get away from this horrid creature. But my legs wouldn't move. I hated Aunt Dede for bringing me here. And then I was looking at Michael, at his eyes, bright blue, but sad—dull, I thought, with no shine. Why had God let this happen to him? Why wouldn't Jesus forgive us both and restore our looks?

"I know I'm ugly," he said, "but the doctors are working on that."

"I . . . I'm sorry, Michael."

"It's okay. Can I touch your hair? It looks soft, and the color reminds me of a raven's wing."

Somehow, I managed a weak smile. And I didn't mind as his stubby, twisted fingers stroked my hair. "You should enter your painting in a contest," I told him. "I'm sure you'd win."

"Thanks," he said. "But I have other plans for it. And thanks for coming to see me, too. It's lonely here."

We left shortly. I didn't say anything all the way home. It didn't seem fair that Michael should be so ugly, and I thought God had certainly made

40

a lot of mistakes. Why did there have to be so much pain and suffering?

Just before Christmas vacation, Mr. Anders brought the *Review* staff to the library to talk about the class project. Every year, each class picked something to do for the school. I wasn't interested. It usually meant doing something dumb, like making posters. I hid behind the largest dictionary I could find, hoping they'd forget about me.

Paige Demson suggested a tree for the courtyard. She was the class president and wanted a project that would interest everyone. Paige's blonde hair looked nice with her navy blue blazer, but her nose was too big.

Wendell mentioned that the Mental Health Players were coming in March, and Paige cut him off. "Not again," she said. "Everyone made posters last year, and no one's very interested in mental health anyway."

Mr. Anders cleared his throat and told Wendell to go on with his idea. But as soon as Wendell got to the part about Drug Awareness Week, everyone groaned.

41

This is dull, I thought. These guys were the brains in our class. Not much to look at, but they got things done. I didn't belong in this group; most of all, I didn't want to, either.

Then Mr. Anders asked, "Wendell, what did you have in mind?"

"A club," he said, grinning. "Like the S.A.D. at the high school. My dad thinks it's a good idea to warn kids about drinking."

"We don't have a drinking problem in Hill View," Jill Taylor grumbled, chewing on her pencil.

"Yes, we do," Allison Corbett said softly. "I agree with Wendell. What do you think, Holly?"

I wanted to fall through the floor! "S.A.D. stands for Students Against Drinking," I mumbled. "But there's nothing sad about kids who drink. It's their own stupid fault."

Heads turned, Allison's eyes filled with tears, and I felt about as wanted as a kid with leprosy. Someone was talking again, but I didn't wait to listen. I couldn't get out of there fast enough. Why me, Lord, I thought, dashing for the door.

"Wait! Holly, wait up!" Allison caught up with me on the corner. "Let me explain about . . . "

"Explain what?" I snapped. "I can't help the way I feel. And you didn't have to drag me into it in the first place!"

"But . . . you don't understand," she began.

"I understand enough! The minute I opened my mouth, they all glared at me like I had two heads. I felt like a jerk!"

"My little brother died last year because he was drunk," she blurted out. "Timmy was only nine, but he was trying to act big. He fell in the creek and drowned. The others knew. That's why they glared at you."

"Gosh, Al, I . . . " and I really felt like a jerk then.

We crossed Springfield and walked down Inwood in silence. When Allison stopped at her house, I asked, "Is your brother the reason Wendell wants a club at school?"

"Wendell just wants to please his father. Dr. Bressler works at Tall Oaks Abuse Clinic," she explained.

That sounded gruesome to me. I didn't even know that Wendell's father was a doctor. Right then I realized that I didn't know any of these kids at all. That made me wonder if they knew me.

6
The
Professor

Allison was staring right past me with a far-away look in her eyes. I felt uncomfortable and shivered, hunching my shoulders inside my jacket. Then she blinked. "Mr. Anders said we can put the club idea on our list if we make it fit everyone. Would you help us make plans?" Her eyes looked hopeful.

I shifted my books against one hip. "What sort of plans?"

"Like a name. Maybe come up with some ideas for raising money—stuff like that."

"Money?" I frowned. "What for?"

"We only have $5.34 from last year. That's not even enough for poster paint. Please help, Holly."

I said I'd have to think about it, and started home. A light, cold mist was falling from a gray sky. Definitely not tennis shoe weather, I thought, staring at my wet toes. When I trudged into the kitchen, I found a note from Aunt Dede.

Working the late shift. Be back at six. Put the casserole in at 350 degrees at 5:15. Love ya!

After preheating the oven, I kicked off my soggy sneakers and went to wash my cold feet. Slumped on the edge of the tub, I relived the afternoon. I felt like a failure. Especially after my blunder over Allison's brother. God had not only made me ugly, He'd allowed me to make a fool of myself. I felt more awkward than ever and I hoped Allison would forget about me.

By Friday, when Aunt Dede took me Christmas shopping, I'd forgotten all about the class project. We were picking out a new necktie for Dad when I saw Kelliann. I waved and smiled. She was riding the escalator, and I know she saw me, too. Kelliann looked right at me. Then she put her nose in the air and stared straight ahead. That's when I decided to help Allison and Wendell with the club.

Saturday I went to the public library. Miss Talbot, the librarian, gave me a stack of free stuff from *Hazelden* and *Al-Anon*. Then she started bringing medical journals to my table.

"This isn't working," I told her. "The eighth grade needs a project to help kids. But not just the ones who drink. Maybe some kind of club."

"Oh, my!" She looked startled. "You should visit with Professor Hillery, dear." Miss Talbot bustled away, returning with a tiny bent old man who carried a cane. He had white hair and his twinkling icy-blue eyes peeked over the metal rims of his glasses. Father Time, I thought, smiling.

"Might I be of service, young lady?" he asked crisply, perching on the edge of a chair beside me.

"I don't know, sir," I admitted, hiding my cheek behind my hand. Then I told him about the project and Allison's brother, trying to sound as grown-up as possible. He folded his hands over the head of his cane, and closed his eyes. I thought he'd fallen asleep. Just as I was beginning to wonder about him, he looked at me sharply.

"The biggest problem here is communication," he said. "Indeed! More people should talk to each other. It might keep our youth out of trouble. You talk, don't you?"

I nodded, said, "Uh, huh," like I'd seen Mom do, then asked, "What do you mean?"

"Suppose Johnny has a problem." And he grinned at me. "His mom's at work, and his dad's sleeping. So who's Johnny going to talk to about his problem?"

"His friend," I suggested. That sounded like a mature statement to me.

"Aha! But who's Johnny's friend? Is it the guy on the corner selling drugs? Or the older kid who just swiped a fifth of booze from his old man?" He wiggled his shaggy eyebrows.

" 'Course not!" I said a little too loudly for a library. "With friends like that, Johnny's in trouble."

"Exactly! Now suppose Johnny had someone his own age who would listen to his problem. Notice I said *listen*. There is not much listening going on these days. Folks are too busy flapping their own jaws to listen." He winked at me like a wise little owl.

"But what about Johnny's problem?" I asked.

"Hang the problem!" he said sternly. "He'll probably work that out on his own. Listening to Johnny is the most important thing, not solving his problem." The professor closed his eyes, and I waited. But when he didn't continue after a long silence, I got worried.

"Is that it?" I asked.

"That's enough," he answered. "You figure it out."

7
The Wrong Number

It was cold outside when I left the library. I started jogging—running helped me think, and there was a lot to think about after talking to the professor. I couldn't wait to tell Allison about him. The minute I got home, I grabbed the phone.

"This is Holly," I said, still breathless from jogging. "Listen, Allison, I think I've got an idea."

"So have I, kid," a voice barked in the receiver.

Like an idiot, I'd dialed the wrong number. Kelliann's phone number was so fixed in my mind that my fingers forgot to listen to my brain. "Sorry," I mumbled. "Wrong number."

"You can say that again," she shouted. "I'm not Allison, but I get the message!" And she hung up.

I was staring at the receiver as if it had bitten me when Aunt Dede stopped puttering in the kitchen. "Did you make a mistake?" she asked.

"Kelliann will think I did that on purpose," I said, choking back my tears. "She thinks the kids on the *Review* staff are a bunch of dipsticks. How come everybody thinks you have to be beautiful to be worth anything?"

Aunt Dede started to say something, then shook her head.

I went up to my room to think. Anyone can make a mistake. But Kelliann, of course, wouldn't know about that. There was something I wanted to remember about my visit with the professor, but thanks to Kelliann, I was no longer in the mood. Instead, I just felt lonely.

Our class picture was on my bulletin board. The really nice-looking kids were easy to find— Kelliann with her shining red hair, or Hank with his toothpaste grin—but the rest were just background. My fingers traced the welt along my cheek. That's where I belonged now, I thought, in

51

the background. Tonight the whole class would have fun at the Sno-Ball party, but *not* me.

The journal from Aunt Dede was on my desk. Maybe this was a good time to start using it.

First, I wrote down all about how Kelliann was being so mean about everything. Next, I tried to write about how God had deserted me, how He'd taken back His gift by turning me ugly. But that made me cry and I had to go splash cold water on my burning eyelids.

The water didn't help, so I went downstairs to help with supper. Aunt Dede was making soup. No one likes soup as much as she does. "I met an interesting man today," I said as I took the soup mugs out of the cupboard. "He said people don't listen to each other anymore."

"That's nice," she said, studying her recipe card.

"I told him about the drinking problem in our school. I wonder why I never saw it before?"

"You were too busy to look." Aunt Dede didn't sound very interested. She kept tasting and stirring the soup.

"Well, don't you think kids should be warned about drinking?"

Aunt Dede looked surprised, then frowned at me. "Sometimes too much awareness works against you, Holly. People have been warned about smoking, but they still smoke. One lady told me that all birth certificates should be labeled to read, 'Caution: Living Is Dangerous to Your Health!' Can you believe that?"

I chuckled. "Well, I think Wendell's right. A club at school would be a good way to help kids."

"Be careful," she warned. "You could end up making enemies. Didn't you tell me this club had to fit everyone?" She ladled soup into the mugs and sat down.

"But Professor Hillery said listening was a good . . . "

"Professor who?" Aunt Dede looked startled.

"Professor Hillery," I said. "He was at the library. I told him about Allison's brother and our class project."

"Oh, that's just great," she said, disgusted. "Now he'll think every child in Hill View is an alcoholic. I can't believe you'd bother such a brilliant man."

"It was Miss Talbot's idea," I said defensively. "The professor didn't seem to mind. Besides, I need all the help I can get, now that Kelliann's being so hateful. She won't even look at me now that I'm ugly."

"Nonsense," she said sternly. "And another thing. If you try teaching kids something for their own good, they won't thank you for it."

"What's that supposed to mean?"

"I just don't want to see you hurt, honey."

"I'm already hurt," I said. "Hank butchered my face, and now you don't want me to have any friends at all."

"You're exaggerating and you know it," she said in that quiet, controlled voice of hers. "I can't blame Kelliann for being upset after the way you acted. Are you trying to force your friends to be something *you* want?"

"No, but . . . "

"Hold it right there, Holly. Friends must be accepted as is. No buts about it. If you have such a passion to help someone, consider those who are nearest to you. Jesus promised us the Holy Spirit so that we could love our neighbors. Well, Hank is your neighbor. If I were you, I'd try showing that love by being nicer to him."

"Well, I'm not you!" I yelled. "You're against

my idea before you've heard it. Why won't you listen? I wouldn't be in this mess if Hank hadn't scarred my face—and you make it sound like I'm the one who hurt *him!*" I ran to my room and slammed the door so hard that the pictures on my wall rattled.

Aunt Dede was right behind me. "I want to tell you . . . "

"I'm not listening!" I snapped, shoving the pillow over my head. "Just go away and leave me alone."

"I'll tell you anyway." She sat on the edge of my bed. "Once there was a brilliant man who tried to teach people in his own village. It was a small village, and everyone knew this man when he was a little boy. They resented his teaching because they knew him too well. Even though he spoke the truth, they all ignored him."

"That's pretty dumb," I mumbled under the pillow. "If he knew what he was talking about, then the people were jerks for not listening. He should've ignored them, too."

"He couldn't ignore them because he loved them so much. He never gave up trying to help or teach them the right way."

Taking my head out from under the pillow, I asked, "So? What's the point? I care, and I'm trying to help, too."

"If someone doesn't want to listen, talking to him is like talking to a stone wall. There are other ways to teach."

"Hey! If I saw Al about to get run over by a speeding car, I'd shout," I said. "And she'd better *listen,* or she'd get smeared. Oh, I know what you're thinking. It's that thing about setting an example."

"Mmm."

"But sometimes that doesn't work," I complained.

Aunt Dede smiled. "When your dad was a little boy, he lost his temper and broke one of my horse statues. Then he began to cry. I hugged him and told him I was sorry."

"That doesn't make any sense!" I said. "Why did you apologize? It was your horse."

"He knew how much that horse meant to me, and he was sorry for what he'd done. But I knew I loved my brother more than that little horse, and I didn't want him to cry—and I was sorry for let-

56

ting him think that I loved the little horse more than I loved him."

She waited, but when I didn't say anything, Aunt Dede went downstairs. After a while, I went down to help with the dishes. "I'm sorry," I apologized, picking up the dishtowel. "That man in the village was Jesus, wasn't it?"

Aunt Dede grinned, and winked at me.

8
The Chestnut Roast

I've always loved a white Christmas, but Mother Nature had dumped two feet of snow on us. I thought that was overkill. Mom and Dad called to say their flight home had been cancelled. Of course, they decided to stay on the sunny beaches. I couldn't blame them.

Aunt Dede and I walked to church with the snow squeaking under our boots. Everything was so quiet and sparkling that for the first time I really understood when we sang *Silent Night, Holy Night.*

After Christmas, the snow trucks came down our street and stacked a mountain of ice chunks in front of our driveway. They sprayed black cinders everywhere, making a generally mucky mess out of the pretty snow—just like Hank had done to my face.

I curled up on the sofa in front of the fire with my journal. Michael had given me his painting, and every time I tried to write about the way I felt, thoughts of him kept getting in the way. After staring at his red poppies for a long time, I titled my journal "Once Upon an Accident" and wrote two pages about Michael and the fabulous talent God had given to him.

That's how I found Aunt Dede's note tucked between the pages. It was a quote from Colossians. *Bear with each other and forgive whatever grievances you may have against one another. Forgive as the Lord forgave you.* She means Hank, I thought, and I wanted to ask her about that—but when she came into the room, my thoughts shifted to the long-handled wire basket she was carrying and the funny smile on her face.

"Why don't you call Kelliann and roast chestnuts?" she suggested. "It's such fun. I know you'd both enjoy it."

I shook my head. "Kelliann should call me first."

"Whatever for? You're the one who lost your temper."

I watched the bluish flames dance across the log. My words had been said; I couldn't take them back. "If I apologize, she'll think I'm a jerk."

"Everyone makes mistakes, Holly. Kelliann will understand, and I'm sure Hank will, too."

I shot a surprised look in her direction, but her back was turned. Maybe Hank did feel rotten about what he'd done. But if I went around telling everyone how sorry I was that they felt bad about my mutilation, they'd think I was a candidate for the funny farm. "I think I'll call Allison and Wendell," I said. "We need to make plans for the new club." This time I dialed very carefully.

Wendell, Allison, and I sat on the floor. For a while there was only the hiss of chestnuts from the basket and the munch of eating the sweet, hot meat dipped in fresh butter.

"We need a lot of money," Al said at last. "Pop

called it 'working capital,' and he suggested a car wash. That glop they put on the roads during winter sure messes up car paint."

"What about a bake sale?" I asked.

Wendell nodded. "Yeah! And the principal might let us use the gym for a rummage sale, too."

It sounded like a lot of work to me. "If the whole class is helping, why do we need so much money?" I asked.

Aunt Dede, who was bringing in hot cider, answered, "It's a good idea to have a fat treasury for the unexpected."

"Right," agreed Wendell. "We'll need to advertise, too."

I chuckled. "Is radio time okay, or would you want a full page ad in the *Star Ledger*?"

Wendell's big ears turned red. "That's not what I had in mind," he corrected, cleaning his glasses on his shirt. "We still need a name, but the gang should listen when we . . . "

"Wait!" I cried and quickly told them about my visit with the professor. "A listening club would be for everyone—and you don't need a problem to talk. Sometimes it's nice just to have a friend who will listen." My words turned my mind to Kelliann.

She used to be my friend, I thought, but she never listened. I wondered why.

Wendell was grinning. "Great! Listening will fit in with alcohol abuse, too." He dug a folded paper out of his back pocket. It was part of the home quiz from The National Institute on Drug Abuse, sent to his father. "Listen to this: 'The most commonly abused substance in the United States is marijuana, alcohol, cocaine, or heroin.' What's the answer, Holly? You gotta pick one from the list."

"Uh . . . cocaine?" I shrugged. "I'm only guessing."

"The answer's on the back," he said.

Al turned the paper over. "*Alcohol!*" she cried. Then she read, " 'About half of all junior high students have tried some type of alcoholic drinks.' " She shuddered. "I can't believe it!"

"I can," Wendell said. "I hear it from Dad all the time. Kids who get hurt from burns and falls or drown have usually been dri . . . "—and his voice trailed away as he glanced at Al.

For a minute there, I was afraid she might cry about her brother, but she smiled. "I miss

Timmy a lot," she said, "but talking about him helps."

Things were getting uncomfortable. Studying my fingernails, I thought the subject needed changing. "Not all kids get into trouble. If I ran a newspaper, I'd dig up every story I could find about kids doing something positive."

"Hey!" Wendell sat up excitedly. "Kids for Positive Listening! How's that for a name? What does K-F-P-L spell?"

I made a face at him. "Nothing, and I can't even pronounce it. Why?"

"Students Against Drinking spells 'sad.' Our club's name should spell something, too!"

Aunt Dede stopped pretending not to listen, and giggled. "It's called an acronym," she said. "These days it's very popular to make a word from the first initials of a name. You kids are on the right track, but don't dwell on alcohol. I'm sure that would turn the others away from your club."

We talked some more about the professor, and then we agreed a listening club was the best. Wendell wanted more about the alcohol abuse thing, only Al squashed that. "If everyone thinks it's only for kids who drink, no one will use the Listening

Post. Let's think about it. Something'll turn up."
She looked at Aunt Dede and grinned shyly.

Our meeting was over when Hank showed up
with his shovel to clear the driveway. I hadn't noticed when Aunt Dede phoned him, and I wasn't
too happy about it. When he finished, Aunt Dede
insisted that *I* give him the money. Yucksville!

"How's it going?" he asked me, staring at the
zipper on his ski jacket and stomping snow from
his boots.

"Okay," I said.

It felt weird talking to Hank. "Are you . . . uh
. . . going out for wrestling?" I asked.

"I guess," he shrugged. Then Hank's eyes
looked right into mine. "Gee, Holly, I'm really
sorry," he whispered.

"It's okay," I said and quickly added, "just
don't make me giggle in Old Lady Pearsall's his-
tory class. I'm on her list as it is."

Hank's grin spread slowly. "You're okay," he
said. Then, bouncing off the porch, he tossed a
snowball at me, adding, "For a jerk, that is!"

Things were okay between us again, and I
prayed. *Thank You, God.* That made me feel good.

I wrote all about Hank in my journal—and about the listening club, too. If I'd listened to Hank a long time ago, this happy feeling would've come sooner. Now we needed a great name for the club. That was the tricky part. Most of the really catchy names were already taken. This was going to take some serious thinking. And my eyes focused on Michael's lovely painting.

As I lay in bed that night, I got to thinking about God. Maybe things were getting better. I had lost Kelliann and Hank, but Hank was my friend again. And, God had given me new friends in the club. Maybe Jesus was forgiving me for whatever after all.

9
The Doodled Picture

We forgot about the club when Mom and Dad came home. They were all excited about their trip, and, over a big turkey dinner, they had to tell us all about sailing in the Bahamas.

Then we opened the gifts they'd brought, and I showed them Michael's painting. Dad was certain he'd seen that beach before, but he couldn't remember where. Mom gave me a sea shell like the one in the painting. We all took turns holding it against our ear to hear the purr of the ocean. Dad liked the tie I gave him, and he made a lot of silly comments about ties in general.

We had a lot of fun the next few days, and before I knew it, Aunt Dede went home, vacation was over, and school was starting.

The project assembly was Monday. I sat with Al and Wendell, doodling in my notebook with my head down. That made my hair fall across my ugly cheek. Paige was explaining her tree idea for the courtyard when Al whispered, "What are you drawing?"

"A sail boat," I whispered back. "I've never been sailing, but it sounds like fun." I wrote the word *Sail* on the triangle above my boat. Al chuckled and scribbled waves on my picture.

Then Wendell nudged me and reached over to draw a fin sticking out of the water. I wrote *Beer* on the fin, and we all giggled. Al drew another shark with his mouth open and wrote *Smoking* between the sharp teeth. Corin was smoking, I remembered, when she burned down her garage. Would she have done that if she'd had someone to talk to, I wondered.

Danny Adams started explaining the sports banner for the gym, and I noticed lots of kids were scribbling in their notebooks. Was anyone listening? I'd read in the Bible that God's voice was a "gentle whisper," but you had to be still to hear it. Hearing is one of God's precious gifts. I wrote *LIS-TEN* at the top of my club notes, then drew a sun around the word with rays touching the sail on my little boat. My attention was suddenly drawn to something Mr. Anders was saying. "Hollis Manning will tell you about the listening club." My stomach dropped right down to my toes.

My knees were shaking, but somehow I made it to the front. It was scary. I looked at my notes. "There's danger everywhere," I began, and someone in front yawned. "Dangers lurk around like sharks. What we need to do is listen to each other."

Somebody giggled, so I spoke louder. "It's bad enough without making trouble for yourself. But if we're aware of the dangers, then the sailing will be easier." Why was I saying this? I stared at my notes. That dumb doodle picture was messing up my brain. Then I got scared, 'cause I knew I'd be graded on my talk. Someone yelled from the back, "Does listening help us sail over stormy waves?" —and there was a lot more giggling.

My cheeks flushed, and I prayed, *Get me out of this, Lord!* Aloud I said firmly, "Yes, it does! Especially when you want to talk, and you need someone to listen. This club is for you, for all Students Aware in Life: S-A-I-L. If you vote for your own club, you'll be sailing with your own friends." Then I hurried to sit down while everyone clapped politely.

Wendell was grinning, and Al was positively beaming when she squeezed my hand. "What a terrific name, Holly. How'd you ever think of that?" she asked. Instead of answering, I showed her the picture we'd drawn. After the class assembly voted, the *Hill View Review* staff gathered in the art room to wait for the results. I was staring out of the window at the snow melting into muddy puddles on the football field. Why did I have to explain the club? It was Wendell's idea first. If the club didn't win, now it would be all my fault.

Paige came over and said, "I like the name of the club, Holly. Was that your idea?"

I shrugged. "It just came out when I started talking," I told her. "Your idea about the tree was good, too. Will you work with us if the club's picked?"

"Sure." Paige smiled. "God takes a long time to make a tree, but He might work faster when it's something important. If the name just came out like that, maybe . . . "

Mr. Anders interrupted as he shoved through the swinging doors, waving a wad of papers. "Okay, okay!" he shouted for attention. "Listen up, gang. The club won the vote. Thanks to Holly, *SAIL* has come to Hill View Junior Academy."

Everyone was cheering and looking at me, and I still didn't know what I'd done. I escaped by going to wash my burning face.

Mr. Roldan, the principal, wanted to see us before we left school. He took us to the room across from his office. "This was a counseling room," he said, standing aside for us to enter. "*SAIL* might like it for their listening post."

"I like the couch," Al said.

Wendell nodded, "We'll need more chairs, I think. What do you say, Holly?"

I looked at the pale-blue carpet, the big window, and the soft couch with its multi-blue striped pillows. "It's not what we want," I said. "Is there another room we could see?"

Wendell groaned. "For pity's sake, Holly, what's wrong with this room?"

71

"Perhaps if I knew what you had in mind," Mr. Roldan said.

Al tugged on my arm. "I really like it."

"No, you don't," I said. "It's too close to the office."

Mr. Roldan smiled. "I think I understand."

We followed him down the hall with our footsteps echoing loudly, and stopped at a door behind the gym. "It's small," he said, fumbling with a ring of keys. "I'm afraid it will need work. We haven't used it for some time."

The door creaked open and Al turned pale. "Gag," she whispered. "I'm sick!"

"You've got to be kidding," Wendell said, leaning against the wall. "This was the janitor's closet! I've seen postage stamps larger than that window."

"It's perfect!" I cried. "It's just what we want."

And Mr. Roldan went down the hall shaking his head while Wendell glared at me in disgust.

10
The Problems

Mr. Anders gave us a small table in the corner of the art room for a command post. Al told everyone about the janitor's closet, and Wendell wrote ads for the *Review,* asking for help. Jill and Trish Lee made sign-up sheets and posted them all around school. The whole class was involved, of course, but the staff members were appointed to head the work committees. My job turned out to be the bake sale.

Valentine's Day was the best, and I made out a work schedule. I wanted donations from everyone. "I don't know," Danny said, frowning. "My mom sure gets tired of baking stuff all the time."

"Get something from a bakery, then," I suggested.

Just then Mark Downs dashed in. "Look!" He was waving a green paper. "This notice went home with the elementary kids. They'll bring extra money and buy goodies from the bake sale for their lunch."

"That's great," said Wendell, smiling at me. "Way to go, Holly!" That made me feel like I belonged.

Brownies always made a big hit. I baked three dozen—some without nuts—and Mom drove me to school early on the morning of our sale. Al was already standing behind the long table in the hall. She looked worried. "We might have a problem, Holly."

"How can we have a problem?" I asked. "Just look at all this yummy stuff. Cakes . . . pies . . . even homemade bread!"

"That's just the point. Little kids don't want a whole pie, and there aren't enough cookies."

"Maybe I can help," Mom said. She was looking over all the delicacies. "I'll get some paper plates, and . . . Oh! Look at this pineapple upside-down cake! It's my favorite, and I never have time to make it. How much do you want for it?"

Al chewed her lower lip. "I'm . . . I don't know, Mrs. Manning. Half this stuff isn't priced yet."

Mom dug into her purse. "I'll give you $10 for it. The dear soul who spent so much time making it would feel cheated if it sold for less."

Danny was behind the table drooling, and the sale hadn't even started. "How much for a brownie?" he asked.

"A quarter," I said. "Where are the stick-on tags, Al? I'll help you price things." Suddenly the homeroom bell rang. Everyone scattered. "Mom!" I wailed. "I've gotta go. Who's going to manage this table?"

"Go ahead," she said. "I'll stay until someone relieves me. Where's your work schedule?"

"Here," I said, shoving the list at her. "Thanks, Mom. Trish should be along any minute." Mom was swell. I could always count on her. But when I came to the table during my free period, she was still there. "What's wrong?" I asked, dropping my books against the wall. "Didn't Trish show up?"

"Trish came and so did Jill. But things got too busy for them to handle alone."

Then Mrs. Downs brought her first grade down the hall. Those bright little faces looked so eager, and I was afraid they'd be disappointed. But Mom cut berry pies and sold each slice for 50 cents. More cookies arrived before the second lunch; cup cakes, too. Later, Mom told me that each person who brought something to sell ended up taking goodies home. By three o'clock we only had crumbs left. And one very tired mom.

On Friday I gave Mr. Anders the money. "We made $63," I said proudly. "That'll buy a lot of poster paint!" Secretly I was very glad my part of this whole thing was over.

Mr. Anders nodded, then reminded us of the Spring Arts Festival coming after Memorial Day. "Parents will want to visit our Listening Post after the awards. We'd better make a list of what is needed, and then set our goal." He wrote my $63 on the chalkboard in the plus column, and each committee gave their report.

"My dentist has an old sail," Mark reported. "That can be our sign. But he wants $10 for it."

Jill raised her hand. "I found bright blue cloth for $5, and my mother will help me sew the word

SAIL on the canvas. But I'll need a design for the letters."

That's when Paige volunteered *me* for the letter design. "You're good at that sort of thing, Holly," she said. Then she told us about the floor pillows at Ferguson's. "They're really nice, but they cost $40 a pair."

The minus column kept growing longer, and I slouched down in my seat. An old, used desk would cost $20; primer and paint would cost $35; brushes and scrapers would cost another $25. I groaned. This was getting depressing.

"Don't forget the car wash," Al said brightly. "And the rummage sale will help, too. Danny's offered us his garage."

"Are we selling Danny's garage?" Mark asked seriously.

Everyone laughed until Wendell stood up. "The listening room has a hole in the wall," he said. "The sink needs to be taken out, too. Leaking water has ruined the floor. . . " When the gang started grumbling, he blushed and sat down.

"Hold on, guys," Mr. Anders said. "We've got two months. With the entire class on this project,

I think we'll make it. Here's our goal." He wrote a big fat $300 on the chalkboard and circled it.

When I started home, I felt like I was dragging two lead blocks instead of feet. How could we raise that much money? I had a book report due in English and a music assignment on *Carmen*. I couldn't just ignore my homework.

The phone was ringing when I opened the back door. It was Jill, and she sounded out of breath. "Ferguson's is having a two-for-one sale," she panted. "Quick, Holly. We can get four pillows!"

"That's great! But why call me?"

"Allison's not home, and I need that 40 bucks now," she cried. "Ferguson's might sell our pillows!"

"Sit on them if you have to," I told her. Then I jogged over to Al's house. Mrs. Corbett told me the money was in a box on Al's desk. I counted out $40, left Al a note, then ran all the way to town. How in the world did I get mixed up in this? At this rate, I sure wouldn't get sneered at for having *good* grades!

11
The Storm Drain Monster

Most of our snow disappeared in March. I enjoyed walking to school in the soft wind, half-listening to Al discussing the pros and cons of getting her hair cut. Al was fun to be with.

One afternoon, I found Al waiting at my locker. "Ready for work?" she asked, wiggling a four-inch paint brush under my nose.

She'd managed to talk me into helping her paint the old, used desk. "I've got to take the design for our SAIL letters to Jill first. Meet you in the art room," I called, dashing for the sewing room.

Things had been running smoothly with everyone working together. But when I got back to the art room, I walked in on an argument.

"No, I already did that!"

"Why? I'm poster chairman."

"Who's collecting stuff for the rummage sale?"

"Not me! I'm sanding the door to that ugly closet!"

And that's when I opened my big mouth. "Who's in charge of this project anyway? Every ship needs a captain."

Things got quiet. They all looked at me. I sure don't remember any voting, but all at once *I* was ship's captain. When I started complaining about my busy schedule, Mr. Anders told me to "delegate responsibility"—and that's how I ended up with a free Saturday. I'd put two teams out scouring for junk to sell and told Wendell to take charge of the car-wash detail.

It had been a long time since I'd talked to Aunt Dede, so that Saturday I took the bus to Sterling and walked the three blocks to her house.

"Hello there, Merry Sunshine," she said when she opened the door. "You're just in time for cranberry juice."

Flopping into the lounger on her back porch, I brought her up to date on the project, ending with, "So I was hoping you might have some ideas for making money."

"Aha! So you came all the way to Sterling just to pick my brain," she said, chuckling.

"Why not?" I grinned at her. "I also wanted to ask about Michael. Whenever I look at his painting, I wonder how he's doing. Is he okay?"

"Michael needs another skin graft, but he's fine; and he's surprising everyone with his progress in therapy. Now, about your problem. Have you ever considered spending money to make money?" she asked, winking.

I groaned. "We're too busy trying to hang on to what we have. Everytime I turn around, Wendell finds something else wrong with our office."

Aunt Dede pointed to where she'd been potting bulbs, saying, "Small peat-pots are reasonable. How about bright blooming plants decorated with foil and ribbons? Sell them in the neighborhood before Easter. Fifty cents would make them cheap enough for children to buy. They'd love it."

"You're terrific," I said, giving her a big hug.

"I know," she chuckled softly. "Plus, I'll do

anything for a hug. A hug a day keeps the doctor away!" Then she drove me home since she needed to run errands.

Al thought the plant idea was great. She called some of the kids who hadn't helped yet, and we were making plans in my driveway when Aunt Dede returned with two flats of bright orange marigolds—and Hank. "Look who I found to help," she called, backing into the drive.

She said the flowers were her donation since she'd missed the bake sale, but I was so shocked watching Hank unload the potting soil and plants I forgot to thank her. Hank? Fooling around with plants?

Everybody got busy, and it took all day to separate and re-pot all those marigolds. The kids got hot and started fussing about dirt under their fingernails, but not Hank. He worked until we were finished. That surprised me. Especially when he said, "Whatever we don't sell we can take to the car wash next weekend. I'll bet they'll sell there."

I ended up with two dozen to sell and stored them in the garage. On Saturday morning I went across the street to ask Gina for her wagon. "Sure, you can use it," she said, putting one hand on her hip like her mother did. "But I get to come!"

Gina was seven, but I needed her wagon. I didn't exactly dislike her, but Gina could be a real pain. She never stopped talking. I was totaling profit in my head when she stopped pulling the wagon and scowled at me. "C'mon," I called. "We have another block to go."

"But you didn't answer," she whined.

"Sorry," I mumbled, sighing. "What did you ask?"

"I didn't ask you anything!" she yelled. "I told you."

"So, what did you tell me?"

"There's a monster living in the drain." I was trying not to laugh when Gina added, "He's all slimy and covered with hair."

Gina's wild imagination, I thought, but I decided to go along with her so I could sell the rest of my plants. "Does your monster have a name?" I asked, pretending to be interested.

"He's not *my* monster!" She stamped her feet. "Monsters are yucky. Sometimes he groans, but today he's crying."

"Right," I said, thinking to myself that it looked like rain. "If he's crying, he won't bother us; so let's get going."

Gina folded her arms and wouldn't budge. "What if he's crying because he is hungry? What if he wants to eat me up?"

"Don't be silly," I told her crossly, sorry that I'd let her come. I didn't like the color of the sky one little bit. "If you're not coming, I'm going without you." I reached for the wagon handle, and Gina suddenly shrieked.

"I hear him! Right there—in the big pipe. I'm going home!"—and she dashed across the corner lawn, heels flying.

I was staring after her when I thought I heard a muffled cry. The kid was nuts, but now she had me hearing things. Looking through the metal grill over the storm drain, I saw that it was full of soggy dead leaves, but I didn't hear anything. So I went to the car wash.

My last plant sold just as fat raindrops speckled the dusty sidewalk, and put a stop to the car wash. I was halfway home when it started raining harder. Gina's wagon began to fill with water; I was soaked. A muddy river formed in the gutter and tumbled into "Gina's" drain pipe with a gurgle. But the water wasn't all I heard; there was another sound—much louder now. I got down on my knees to listen, hoping no one was watching. They'd think I'd lost my mind for sure.

"Hello!" I yelled into the pipe. "Is anyone there?"

"I'm stuck," answered a small voice.

All at once there was a hard knot in my stomach. We'd been warned about those drains. They filled with water during a storm and ran for miles under the streets before dumping into the river. *What dumb jerk was in there?*

"Come to the opening, I'll pull you out!" I shouted.

"Foot's caught," came the answer. "Hey! There's water in here . . . all over the place. I'm getting awful wet!"

There wasn't time to go home. I ran to the nearest house. Horrid pictures flashed through my mind as I pounded on the door. If only I could pray. But God seemed so unreachable these days. He'd punished me with the ugly scar on my face, and I wasn't sure He was listening to my prayers. It was taking forever for someone to answer the door. My hand touched the doorknob. It turned easily. I couldn't wait any longer. As I opened the door, I wondered what it was like to be arrested for breaking into someone's house.

12
The Rescue

Halfway down the hall stood a tiny old woman. Her gnarled fingers gripped the silver bar of her walker like an eagle's talons. One look at me dripping all over her waxed floor made her bright blue eyes get enormous.

"Emergency," I puffed. "Where's the phone?"

When she pointed toward the kitchen, I dashed past her. The number for the rescue squad was taped to the wall above the phone. I dialed it. While the phone was ringing, I asked the lady for her address. Then a man's voice growled in the ear piece. "Hill View Rescue, Sergeant Dillon."

"This is Hollis Manning," I said in my most

grown-up voice. I didn't want him to think I was some little kid playing a prank. "Please send help to 401 Crestview Drive. A child is stuck in the storm drain on the corner."

"Keep talking to the child," he told me in a concerned voice. "I'll send a city work crew over right away."

After I hung up, I apologized to the lady for dripping on her floor. Then I ran back to the street, my sneakers squishing at every step. *I'm scared, Lord*, I prayed silently. *Please help me!* It didn't take long for the city truck—a big green one—to arrive. Then a police cruiser led the rescue squad's ambulance around the corner.

By this time a lot more water was going into the drain. I sat on the curb and prayed as hard as I knew how. *Please, God. Let these men be in time.*

One of the men used a special hook to lift the metal grating. Another guy climbed down inside and disappeared into the fat, dark pipe. The minutes dragged while I stared at the opening. Then I saw the man's yellow slicker. He backed slowly out of the pipe, dragging little Jake Swenson after him.

I shivered as I watched a man from the ambulance wrap Jake in a blanket. The policeman asked me some questions. I told him what I knew of Jake—not much since he was Gina's age—and where he lived. Jake was strapped onto a stretcher just like they'd done to me. When they drove away, the red light was turning—and I shivered again. Then the policeman was talking.

"That was quick thinking on your part. That kid may very well owe his life to you."

"He'll be okay, won't he?" The officer was tall, and I tipped my head back to see him, letting the rain pelt my face.

"Oh, sure," he said, smiling. "Right now he's wet, upset, and probably cold. If he'd stayed in there much longer ... " He didn't finish his thought.

That suited me fine. I didn't want to hear the gory details. When the policeman went to the lady's porch to talk to her, I followed. It gave me a chance to apologize again for messing up her floor, but she didn't seem to mind once she'd heard about Jake.

The policeman drove me home with Gina's wagon in the back of the cruiser. I peeled out of at least 50 pounds of soggy jeans and sweatshirt.

Lucky for me, Mom wasn't home. Wet clothes always make her nervous.

On Sunday I had a lot of news for my journal. First, I wrote about Hank helping with the flowers. Then I wrote about finding Jake in the storm drain and how scared I'd been. I was sure glad God had listened when I asked him to save that dopey little kid.

Monday afternoon Mr. Anders was pleased when we turned in the money from the plant sale. But Wendell's car wash had closed early because of the rain, and we still had a long way to go. I really wasn't paying much attention; I had brought my journal to write in—a lot more fun. But Danny's high-pitched, whiney voice couldn't be ignored. "My mom says our garage looks like a junk shop. What if that stuff doesn't sell?"

"We'll give the leftovers to charity," Jill told him.

"But we really need to sell everything we can, Danny," Al reminded him.

Danny puffed up like a little toad at all the attention. I made a note to add a page on him in my journal. Then Mark started talking about the bike-a-thon. "Pledges are a great way to make money," he said. "Maybe we could do something like that."

"Yeah," agreed Wendell. "How about running laps or something? We've still got to pay for the plumber."

I frowned. "That's no good. Some kids don't like running. It should be something everyone likes to do."

My saying that made Paige grin. "Thanks, Holly. If I don't keep everyone happy, they yell at me a lot. Besides, most people are busy on their art projects for the festival."

Just thinking about the festival made me sad. Last year I'd been Girl of the Flowers. Definitely O-U-T for a scarface.

After the meeting, Wendell came up to me at my locker. "Maybe you can think of an idea for this pledge thing, Holly."

"Go soak your head," I said, grinning at him. "I've spent every afternoon in our Listening Post scraping ugly walls. I don't even have anything for the festival. Last year I won a ribbon for my photo of Kelliann and her kittens, but this year . . . " It hurt to talk about it, so I just shrugged.

"Oh, you'll think of something." He chuckled. "You're our captain, and leaders usually have swell ideas!" Then he dashed down the hall before I could throw my math book at him.

Wendell had made me think about Kelliann, and that upset me. This leader thing confused me, too. I was pretty sure it was God's way of punishing me, but I didn't know why. The really hard part of this mess was losing my best friend. It felt like I had a big empty place inside. Once I hadn't talked to Kelliann for a whole week after she'd slopped chocolate syrup on my best sweater. But that was in fifth grade—ages ago. She'd given me her new red marking pen and things were okay after that. But this was different. Kelliann hadn't talked to me for months! Why was she hurting me like this? Maybe I wasn't pretty anymore, but I still felt like the same person.

Maybe, just maybe, I should call her first.

13
The
Unexpected
Publicity

I still hadn't decided about calling Kelliann, so instead I went over to see how Jake Swenson was feeling. He answered the door and said he felt great. Maybe losing my best friend had me in a bad mood, but seeing Jake's silly grin suddenly made me angry. "What were you doing in that drain?" I demanded sternly. "It's dangerous in there."

"I was saving Fred." His grin got bigger.

"You could've been hurt!" I snapped at him. "I'll bet your mom's told you that a hundred times."

"Indeed, I have," a woman's pleasant voice called from inside the house. Then Mrs. Swenson came out. "You saved Jake's life, Holly. We're proud of you, and very grateful!"

I gulped and nodded. I hadn't done anything very special, and it made me nervous to have his mother fussing over me. So, when Jake wanted to show me Fred, I was relieved to follow him into the back yard.

Fred turned out to be a big green frog. "He's a good hopper," Jake bragged. "Scott Brown has a frog too. We play leapfrog with these guys every day. That's how Fred got in the drain. I had to get him out."

I admitted that I used to play leapfrog, but it was the kind where you jumped over another kid. "Just stay out of that drain," I warned him as I started to leave.

When I came around the corner of the house, a man got out of his car. "Just a minute," he called. "I'm Tony Donchez with the *Star Ledger*. May I ask you a few questions?"

He showed me his press card. "I guess so," I said.

"Mrs. Swenson called to say you'd saved her son's life. I'd like to hear more about that." He leaned against his car to take notes.

"It wasn't much," I began. Then I explained about hearing Jake in the drain and calling the rescue squad. That meant I had to tell why I was out in the rain in the first place, and that led to my telling all about our SAIL project.

Mr. Donchez seemed very interested. "The whole eighth grade, eh? Would you mind if I took some pictures?"

"You mean for the newspaper?" The thought surprised me.

"Sure. Folks in this town will be interested in reading about you. This SAIL project sounds interesting, too. It's nice to see young people involved in the community."

Mr. Donchez took his camera out of his car, and I stood beside Jake and his frog. I turned my head so the scar wouldn't show. When he finished taking pictures, I reminded Mr. Donchez it was Professor Hillery's idea about listening. He took more notes about that. Then I thanked him and jogged home.

Being in the newspaper would be exciting, but I decided not to say anything until the story appeared. I was afraid it would sound like I was bragging. Besides, Mom was already frowning over my grades, and Dad lectured me to use my time more wisely.

It was a good thing I'd kept my mouth shut. Once my picture appeared in the paper things went wild!

Mom was delighted when people started calling; I think she liked talking on the phone. It was different with Dad; he frowned a lot.

At supper one night—after another call had interrupted our meal—Dad scowled at me. "You shouldn't have mentioned the professor that way, Hollis. You made it sound like you were good friends."

"He is my friend," I said defensively. Dad never calls me Hollis unless he's upset. But I hadn't done anything wrong.

"Professor Hillery is a very busy man." Dad put down his fork. "One visit does not constitute a chummy relationship. I really wish you'd be more careful of what you say."

"But that's not fair! I didn't say we were chummy." All at once I wanted to turn my back on this whole thing.

"Statements can be misleading," Dad went on. "You know how newspapers have a way of blowing things out of proportion. I just want you to be more careful from now on."

Mom sighed. "Honestly, Frank, you're being a little harsh, I think. Holly just didn't want to take all the credit for that club idea. No real harm has been done, and I'm sure the professor doesn't mind the publicity."

Then Mom was going on and on about how wonderful I was not to have lost my head in an emergency, and how she was getting extra papers to send to all our relatives. Dad listened, of course, but his lips were drawn into a firm line, and I could tell he wasn't thrilled. When he mentioned my dropping grades, I didn't feel very wonderful and went to my room.

At Friday's meeting, I was ready to tell Mr. Anders that Wendell could take over. Before I had the chance, he said, "We'd better talk about this pledge idea."

Several hands shot into the air, and I began making notes in my journal. I could always tell him later.

Trish suggested roller-skating, and Chuck got all excited.

"How 'bout a dollar a pledge for each kid who roller-skates down Diamond Hill Road!"

"You're nuts!" I yelled. "That's the steepest hill in town. Are you trying to kill somebody?"

Wendell chuckled. "You got a better idea, Holly?"

"Yeah!" I crossed my eyes at him. "My idea is that I want out of this project. It's got me so goofy, I just might suggest having the class leapfrog to town for pledges." That sounded so ridiculous to me, I started giggling hysterically.

Wendell's eyes got big, and he sprang to his feet so fast his chair fell over. "Terrific!" he shouted. "Maybe Dr. Evans can pull his boat for us, too. We'll 'Leapfrog for SAIL!' "

I was sure Dr. Evans was too busy being a dentist, but Wendell didn't give me the chance to say so. He yanked me to my feet and started pulling me around the room. Kids in the hall stopped to watch, and I caught a glimpse of coppery-red hair. "Stop it, you wacko!" I cried, pulling free of him.

"But you did it, Holly!" And before I could stop him, Wendell hugged me right there in front of everyone.

14
The
Good-bye

The day of our garage sale was sunny. People starting coming at seven-thirty. Wendell set up a table on the lawn, and Jill taped a poster she'd made on the front: *Leapfrog for SAIL: Students Aware in Life! 50 cents a leap.* Bright green frogs were painted all over the place. Each frog's head was a photo of someone in our class.

When I arrived, the rest of the committee ganged up on me and said that since it was my idea in the first place, I had to sit at the pledge table. Danny found a captain's hat and made me wear it.

People kept coming over saying they'd seen my picture in the paper. They asked questions about SAIL and wrote their names on the sign-up sheets. When we finally closed down the sale, Al reported we'd made over $110 on other people's junk.

When I got home, I noticed the big maple tree was showing signs of life after its long winter's sleep. Tiny green feathers were sprouting from the ends of naked twigs. Then Kelliann came around the corner on her bike. When she saw me, her nose went up in the air, and she turned her head, pretending to be very interested in the dandelions sprouting in Gina's front yard.

I just stared at her—at her small, delicate face, her trim body in its pale-green pants suit, her red hair shining in the sun. It was like seeing for the first time Kelliann's wall of protection from others, her contempt for the cruel thoughts of others who were jealous of her good looks. All at once I was yelling, "I'm not like the others! We can be friends if you want." I ran inside, not daring to look back.

I'd seen that look before—even used it myself—but I'd never been on the receiving end. All at once I realized that the chin up, back-straight swagger wasn't being stuck-up like people thought! It was my way to protect myself so I didn't get hurt. Had I hurt others the way Kelliann had hurt me?

Jesus, I prayed, *please help me! Forgive me for being so blind. Let Your Holy Spirit show me what to do and help me do it. Please give me a chance to forgive Kelliann for hurting me. Give me the wisdom to learn that, because You died for me, I never need doubt Your love for me. Let Your forgiving love for me flow through to Kelliann.*

This was something I wanted to add to my journal, but I couldn't find it. While I was looking, I noticed Michael's painting and got a fabulous idea.

The next morning Dad helped me take the painting down, and I entered it in the Spring Arts Festival. Al thought it was the most beautiful picture she'd ever seen. I told her all about Michael, and she wrote a nice article on him for the *Hill View Review*. I hoped that if everyone knew about Michael they'd give his painting a ribbon, even though he didn't go to Hill View.

At last the horrid janitor's closet was about to become SAIL's Listening Post. Mark asked the art teacher, Mrs. White, to help him with a special project, but he kept it a secret. We finally saw it just before our next meeting. I was shocked! Mark had painted the whole back wall to look like a giant window overlooking a bay with sail boats on the bright, blue water. Even the tiny window was painted to look like part of a sail.

Wendell clapped Mark on the shoulder, saying, "I knew that stamp-size window was good for something!"

Mark grinned at us like he'd just won the gold cup in the Newport Regatta. Al was in top spirits, too. Waving the pledge sheets, she said, "At this rate we'll pay our bills and have money left over. All we need is a date for our leapfrogging."

"I have some good news," Mr. Anders told us, tugging on his beard. "The town council has invited us to leapfrog in the Memorial Day parade, and," he paused to grin, "Dr. Evans has agreed to join us with his boat."

Everyone cheered.

I was so excited Monday morning that I woke

up before the alarm went off. I was waiting for Al under my budding maple tree when a strange car stopped and some guy got out.

"I came to say good-bye, Holly," he said.

"Michael? Is that you?" He was wearing a blond wig.

His fat lips grinned at my surprise. "They matched my own hair color pretty well. Fooled you, didn't I?"

"I'll say. You look terrific!"

Michael explained that his mother had bought a house in Connecticut, near the ocean. His blue, blue eyes were sparkling. "It's right on the beach, and I'm taking art lessons this summer, too," he added excitedly.

"That's great!" I grabbed his hand. "I put your painting in the Arts Festival at my school. Someday when you're a famous painter, I'll be able to brag about knowing you. I'll even own one of your paintings!"

Michael chuckled and squeezed my hand. "And you'll be a famous writer. I'll buy all your books, Holly."

Then we were hugging. I was glad for Michael, but I was sad at the same time. Somehow, I knew

I'd never see him again. The doctors must've worked a miracle on him; Michael wasn't ugly to me anymore. I promised to send him the ribbon if his painting won anything. When I waved good-bye, I felt like I was losing a good friend. This was something special to write about, and I was disappointed that I'd lost my journal.

Zillions of people turned out for the Memorial Day parade. The crowd laughed and clapped as we came leapfrogging down Springfield Avenue behind Dr. Evans and his boat. Our SAIL sign looked great on his mast, the bright blue letters shining on the white canvas. That Monday was a fun day, but the next morning I ached in places I never thought possible.

Limping painfully into homeroom, I collided with Sally Whittle. Books flew in all directions. For a minute, she stared at me with frightened eyes. Then I giggled. "Sorry," I said. "After yesterday, I feel older than Methuselah's grandmother, and blinder than a bat."

"That's pretty gross, Holly." Sally helped me pick up my books. "How do I look without braces?" she asked.

That startled me. "Oh, my! I . . . I didn't notice," I admitted. What was wrong with me? School was almost over for the year, and I felt like I'd been sleepwalking through every class. It was a good thing summer was coming. I really needed a rest.

15
The Different
Kind of Queen

Every light in Hill View High was blazing when we arrived for the Arts Festival. "I'll go park the car," Dad said as Mom and I got out at the door. We walked in and stopped in the hall to look at Michael's painting. A purple ribbon hung from the frame.

"Honorable mention," Mom said. "How nice for Michael."

"Terrific!" I said. "I'll meet you in the Listening Post after the awards are over."

Trish took Mom to find a seat, and I headed

for the SAIL room. It looked great. There were flowers everywhere with tags saying things like "Smooth SAIL-ing, from Hill View Trust" and "Good Listening, from your friends at Wayne's Bakery."

The project was over, and I was suddenly sad. Working on it had been fun. Hard work, of course, but fun all the same. I was thankful I was alone, because I wanted to cry—but Wendell appeared out of nowhere and didn't give me the chance.

"There you are!" he shouted. "We've been looking for you."

I started to protest when he grabbed my hand, dragging me down the hall. But then Hank dashed up with Al right behind him and both were babbling excitedly.

"Your journal about SAIL won the writing award," Al said.

"And you'll never in a million years guess who's here," Hank added. "C'mon, Holly. They're waiting for you."

My heart was pounding. "But . . . my journal wasn't entered. I lost it, and . . . "

Wendell interrupted. "You left the journal in

the library. I figured you'd forgotten, so I entered it for you."

They were pushing me toward the stage. "I'm not going out there. All those people. My face! I can't!"

"The scar's gone, Holly," Hank chuckled.

My fingers touched my cheek—my *smooth* cheek. I started laughing.

Wendell looked puzzled.

The ugly red scar was gone—and I'd never seen it leave. I'd been too busy to look at myself in some dumb old mirror. Silently I prayed, *Thank You, Lord. Please forgive me for being so proud and selfish. I realize now You weren't punishing me, but leading me.*

Then I was on the stage with Mr. Anders shaking my hand. Kathy Parker was Girl of the Flowers, and she pinned blue and white carnations to my dress. Mr. Roldan was speaking into the microphone. "Making the award for sensitivity in writing, chairman of the Child Psychology Department from State University, author of *The Art of Listening to Youth*, it is my great honor to introduce Professor Brainard Hillery."

My knees shook. All those people were clapping, and my insides quivered like jello. I was holding a $100 savings bond, my tears making everything blurry. The professor put his arm around me, and I thought of Dad watching. Now he'd see that the professor was my friend. I wanted to shout, "Hello, world, you're mine!"—but I knew it wasn't. It never had been.

"This bond belongs to SAIL," I heard myself saying. "It's for all Students Aware in Life. Everyone should be up here with me since they helped earn it."

The whole class crowded around—all of them beautiful and talented. The professor whispered to me, "How's Johnny coming with his problem?"

"I'm not sure," I said. "But now that we have the SAIL Listening Post, he'll have a chance to tell me."

"Atta girl, Holly," he said quietly as we left the stage.

The hallway was choked with parents and kids—guys shoving for the punch bowl, girls showing off their projects. I just leaned against the wall, watching, like I wasn't really there. I was remembering how Hank had stuck to the flower job. Jill could sew; Al was great with money; Paige was

113

considerate of others; and they'd made me feel special by choosing me to be their captain. And Wendell had never even noticed my scar! *The real beauty is inside of them* I thought in surprise. *And God planned it that way.* Faces and brightly colored clothing blurred into moving patterns. Suddenly I thought of Michael. Even he was beautiful because of God's gift of talent inside of him. Friends were hugging as soft music from the intercom floated through the voices. SAIL was just beginning, and I was excited about going to high school next year. Maybe SAIL could come, too.

Then I was moving, pushing through the crowd toward a flash of coppery hair, praying in my heart, "*Jesus forgive me. Please heal any hurts I've caused, even when I didn't know I was hurting people. You knew, Lord, the gift of beauty and loveliness, and You shared. Thank You for making me one of Your family by Your death and resurrection. I want to thank You, praise You, and love You— for ever and ever.*"

God had helped me learn that true beauty is using the gifts He has given us for the sake of others—and I had to share that with my best friend, Kelliann.

Love is patient,
Love is kind.
It does not envy,
It does not boast,
It is not proud.
It is not rude,
It is not self-seeking,
It is not easily angered,
It keeps no record of wrongs.

1 Cor. 13:4–5